LITTLE RED RIDING HOOD

Little Red Riding Hood

RETOLD AND ILLUSTRATED BY

Andrea Wisnewski

DAVID R. GODINE · PUBLISHER · BOSTON

First published in 2006
DAVID R. GODINE · *Publisher*
Post Office Box 450
Jaffrey, New Hampshire 03452
www.godine.com

LIBRARY OF CONGRESS CATALOGING-IN-PUBLICATION DATA
Wisnewski, Andrea.
Little Red Riding Hood / retold and illustrated by Andrea Wisnewski. — 1st ed.
p.   cm.
Summary: A version of the classic story about a little girl, her grandmother,
and a not-so-clever wolf, set in nineteenth-century rural New England.
HARDCOVER ISBN 1-56792-303-8 (hardcover : alk. paper)
SOFTCOVER ISBN 1-56792-589-8
[1. Fairy tales. 2. Folklore—Germany.]
I. Little Red Riding Hood English. II. Title.
PZ8.W7539LI 2006
[E]—dc22
2006022122

FIRST SOFTCOVER PRINTING, 2017
Printed in China

FOR CHRIS,
the woodsman who comes to my rescue.

There was once a little farm girl who everyone adored. Her mother and father doted on her but her grandmother loved her to distraction and, not surprisingly, was always making presents for her. One day she made her a cloak as bright as a berry, which suited her so well that everyone called her Little Red Riding Hood from that day forward.

One morning, in the farm-house kitchen, her mother was busy slicing apples and stringing them up to dry by the fire. She said to Little Red Riding Hood, "Go and see your grandmother today for I hear she is feeling poorly and I know you would cheer her up. Take over this basket with the bread I have just made and this fresh pat of butter."

Her mother fastened Little Red Riding Hood's cloak around her shoulders and told her sternly, "Now, walk straight to your grandmother's and do *not* run off the path or you may spill the basket or get lost. When you get there remember your manners and say 'Good morning' and don't go peeping into every corner before you do it."

"I'll take care and be *very* good," the girl promised, kissing her mother goodbye.

Grandmother lived way off in the woods and to get there the girl followed a path her father made with the big wood sled. Before long she saw some bright red winterberries and, tempted to pick a bunch for her grandmother's table, she made her way in the deep snow to pick a nice bouquet. She failed to notice a large wolf watching her from a shadowy thicket.

Suddenly the wolf stepped up and curled his tail around her. Startled to see a wolf so close and not knowing what a wicked creature he was, she was hardly surprised when he said, "Good day Little Red Riding Hood. Where are you going on such a bright morning?"

"To cheer up my grandmother with some warm bread and butter," answered the girl.

The wolf thought to himself, "My, what a tender young creature! I'd eat her now but for those woodsmen close by." Instead he asked, "Where does your grandmother live?"

"On the other side of the wood in the yellow house. Surely you know it," replied Little Red Riding Hood.

"Oh yes," answered the wolf, thinking to himself, "Now I will have two meals instead of one, but I'll have to be plenty crafty to catch them both!"

So when Little Red Riding Hood had finished picking all the berries she wanted and tried to make her way out of the deep snow back to the path, the wolf suddenly had a very wicked idea.

"Hop on my back Little Red and I shall take you back to the path."

"Oh, thank you, kind wolf!"

"What a lamb!" thought the wolf gleefully as he took Little Red Riding Hood's basket in his mouth. "I will take her to the most distant path that leads to her grandmother's house. This is going to be even easier than I thought." And with the girl on his back, he started off through the deep snow.

They reached the path in no time at all, for the wolf knew many short cuts through the woods.

"There you are, Little Red Riding Hood," said the wolf sweetly. "If you stay on this path you won't lose your way again."

"Thank you, wolf," she said and started down the path not noticing that as soon as she turned her back the wolf slid back into the trees and took yet one more of his shortest short cuts through the woods. He had a plan, and he meant to see it through.

The wolf, who handily beat Little Red Riding Hood, ran straight to Grandmother's house and knocked on the door.

"Who is there?"

"Little Red Riding Hood," replied the wolf sweetly. "I'm bringing you some warm bread and butter."

Grandmother, who was in bed, called, "Oh lovely, dear. Just pull the bobbin, lift the latch, and come right on in."

The Wolf, naturally, followed her instructions quite precisely and in a jiffy he was inside the little cottage, quickly making his way to her small bedroom at the back of the house.

The wolf rushed into the room and was at her bedside in a trice. When she saw it was a wolf and not her sweet grand-daughter, she opened her mouth to scream, but the wolf was too quick and ate her up in one gulp. It had been a slim winter and he was eager and very hungry.

Grabbing Grandmother's lace nightcap and spectacles, which had fallen to the floor, the wolf quickly put them on, jumped in the bed, and pulled the covers right up to his chin. Just then he heard a knock on the door.

"Who's there?" rasped the wolf.

Such a rough voice! Her dear grandmother did sound very sick indeed!

"It's your grand-daughter bringing you some warm bread and butter to cheer you up."

Softening his voice the wolf called, "Pull the bobbin and lift the latch dear, for I am sick in bed."

Little Red Riding Hood opened the door to the dark room.

"Close the door, child, the light hurts my eyes!" cried the wolf.

The room became even darker, and she could barely see. Going to the bed, she drew back the curtain. Even by the faint light coming through the window she could see that her grandmother looked very strange indeed! It was the wolf dressed up as her beloved grandmother! A clever girl, she pretended not to notice so she could figure out what to do next. She stalled, saying, "What big ears you have Grandmother!"

"The better to hear you with," said the wolf.

"And Grandmother, what big eyes you have!"

"The better to see you with, my dear child."

"But your mouth is so big and your teeth are so sharp!"

"The better to *eat* you with!" snapped the wolf as he lurched toward Little Red Riding Hood.

But the wolf, sluggish from eating Grandmother, was slow and Little Red Riding Hood was fast. She ran to the door, flung it open and screamed as loud as she could. Luckily her father, passing nearby with a load of wood, heard her cries. He rushed into the house and felled the wolf with a mighty swing of his axe. "I've finally got you, you old devil!"

"I think he ate Grandmother!" cried Little Red Riding Hood.

Carefully slitting open the wolf's stomach they found her, shocked and shaken, but none the worse for wear.

Once she realized she was alive and well, Grandmother forgot her little misadventure, put on her best apron and made tea and hot buttered toast with the gifts from Little Red Riding Hood's basket.

"Oh, Grandmother, I'm so happy that you are all right," said Little Red Riding Hood.

"I'm right as rain thanks to you and your father," she responded pertly, playfully tugging on the girl's blond pigtail. "But I hope to heaven I never see the inside of a wolf again for as long as I live!"

ACKNOWLEDGMENTS

I would like to thank the helpful staff and interpreters at
Old Sturbridge Village in Sturbridge, Massachusetts,
where this tale is loosely set.

An enormous thank you goes to the many people
who purchased prints from this book to help defray costs.
I greatly appreciate your generosity.

Last, but not least, thanks to my daughter Allison
for obligingly posing in a red cape just about anywhere.

DESIGN AND COMPOSITION BY CARL W. SCARBROUGH